TEN DARK STORIES

Ella Low

Image attributions:

Cover: Image by Georgiana Romanovna – GeorgyGirl at https://pixabay.comphotostexture-cracked-antique-sepia-dark-319743 desaturated from original

Page 5: Image by Stefan Keller - Kellepics at https://pixabay.com/illustrations/composing-woman-fantasy-face-2391033 desaturated from original

Page 8: Image by Waldkunst at https://pixabay.com/photos/dark-art-demon-witch-fireball-2838965 desaturated from original

Page 12: Image by Tay.Gun Ozbek at https://pixabay.com/photos/woman-portrait-human-people-old-338321 desaturated from original

Page 14: Image by Enrique Meseguer - Darksouls1 at https://pixabay.com/photos/storm-apocalypse-fantasy-clouds-4047352 desaturated from original

Page 21: Image by Thomas Rudesheim - Sick-Street-Photography at https://pixabay.com/photos/horror-gruesome-scary-halloween-4217529 desaturated from original

I would like to dedicate this volume to some of my fabulous, talented and encouraging musician friends from our lockdown Zoom open mic sessions, whom I often regaled (whether they wanted it or not) with Spoken Word titbits of my dark stories; despite which, they have stayed my friends to this day... In no particular order:

Jill C, Steve A, Steve L, Steve M, Andy G, Beth G, Brian C, David P, Martin T, Kathy J, Pete J, Raph J, Peter C, Debbie C, Geoff Mc, Ann Mc, Enid D, Irene M, Fiona L, and especially to Marilynn K, who sadly is no longer with us.

"A Victorian Funeral" is dedicated to the amazing Jonathan Goodwin, whose voice I channelled when I conjured the narrative.

With many thanks to my friend Kaiti the English teacher, who proof-read and tweaked my use of language.

With lots of love and eternal gratitude to my husband Steve, my rock and number one (or is it the only one?) fan.

Ella xx

Table of Contents

Into the Woods

Nemophilist – (noun) One who is fond of forests or forest scenery; a haunter of the woods

They walked in silence, their unspoken words loud. The woods were eerily quiet, and very little light filtered through the green canopy. The reason for their walk was to *clear the air*, which seemed such a daunting thing to do. Whatever has been, or should have been, whatever it is now, has absolutely no impact on whatever will be. Ever. He knew that well, in fact he knew there was no future for them pretty much from the first couple of days of courtship. On the other hand, she was full of foolish hope. She didn't, she couldn't, she *wouldn't* let go. She begged him to meet her so they could *talk*. He gave in eventually, so he once more lied to his wife about going out for a run in the woods. He now regretted that decision. Not the bit about lying to his wife – he's done this so many times before - but about meeting her again.

He needed to stop this now, for good. Her behaviour has become increasingly erratic since they last met: she would stalk him, follow him, she would attempt contacting him at all hours, even at home. And this will not do. He will need to be firm with her now.

As they walked side by side, she extended her cold fingers, timidly, towards his hand, trying to grasp his hand. He recoiled at her touch, and put his hands in the pockets. Indeed, gone were the days when they would spend illicit afternoons in these very woods, hand in hand, both hungry for each other's touch. She always loved this place; she used to say that she could feel the real magic of the trees, and that it made her love him more. Secluded, dark and not a soul around for miles, these woods have witnessed their passion more times than he was prepared to count. 'You could kill someone here, and nobody would ever know', they used to joke.

'I love you', she said, her big brown eyes filled with sadness. 'I have always loved you… and I always will.'

'I really don't know what else I can say to you' – he was getting quite fed up now, because they had this type of conversation so many times, he lost count. He continued, sharply: 'I told you a million times, it is over, I never loved you, it was just a bit of fun, and you knew the score straight from the beginning. It was never meant to last as long as it did, I have my own life, my family…' he paused to draw breath. 'I have done what you said, you promised me that it would be over, but you didn't keep your side of the bargain! Frankly, I have had enough of you now, I want you to stop following me everywhere, I am sick of you!!'

'So what did I say? What exactly are you referring to? …Bargain? What bargain??' She sounded confused and hurt.

'I only said that I would love you for the rest of my life, and that not even death would stop me from adoring you – it was a figure of speech, for goodness' sake, why did you have to make it all so... literal? How was I supposed to know, I mean how *on earth* was I supposed to know that I would still be madly in love with you, even after you've killed me?? I've never been dead before, and I can't turn my feelings off with the switch of a button!'

She had a point, he thought. But it was still not good enough. He reached the twisted tree, and saw the small mound at its feet. That's where he put the body, after he strangled her. He thought that it would put a stop to all this. She more or less promised him so. It's what she told him.

Yet, five months later, she is still at it.

'Bloody women!!', he spat ruefully.

The Promise

Aeipathy – (noun) An enduring and consuming passion

The old, warty witch was staring at the crowd, through the billowing smoke gathering around her slight body tied to the pyre. Toothless mouths and dirty faces were shouting and chanting, 'Kill the witch! Kill the witch!'

A mob of a hundred or so peasants, ironically innocent in their ignorance, were happy to see her put to death. But she was not afraid. She was not afraid to die, not today, not ever. She was not afraid to feel her flesh in searing pain, as the flames were licking at her bare legs. She knew that He will save her. The beautiful, adorable dark angel who stole her heart – he who promised her life eternal.

He was indeed the most handsome man she has ever met: his fiery eyes, dark and piercing like a black moon's tale. His milky skin, soft like a baby, and smelling of spices and dusk. His mouth, sweet like honey, and lips full, like a forbidden fruit. She gave herself to him when she was young. He entered her body and drilled into her soul, the passion as hot and as consuming as the fires of Hell itself. Just like the merciless flames of the pyre, biting avidly at her thighs and breasts, the melted tallow of her scorching body dripping back into the fire, feeding it into devouring her even faster.

The witch shrieked for help, in her last agonising moments. The pain was so unbearable, and she could no longer see. Her saviour wasn't coming to her rescue, of that she was now certain. Drowning into her own smoke, choking on her flesh's burning fumes, the witch suddenly regretted everything she did. She tried to call for help: she wanted to recant, to repent, to confess, to convert. But her cries were muffled by the fire, and the crowd only cheered her wretched demise. It was too late.

Somewhere in a clearing, a handsome man and a young, rosy cheeked maiden were frolicking in the dewy grass. A steely glint flashed into his dark eyes, as miles away the burning witch was drawing her last tortured breath. He felt his powers strengthening, having claimed yet another wretched soul forever. His luscious lips were shaping the smile of the victor.

'Give yourself to me', he whispered into the girl's ear, his deep and breathy voice sending shivers full of lust down her spine. 'Be mine, all mine... And I shall be yours forever... And I will grant you youth and life eternal... Give yourself to me... Let the fire of your passion burn... Let it burn, my love...'

Perfect Family

Ataraxia – (noun) A state of freedom from emotional disturbance and anxiety; tranquility

I sit here in the semi darkness, looking at my wife cradling our infant daughter, and I smile to myself – how beautiful they both are, how calm and perfect my life is. Our marriage is back on its right track: we have no arguments, no fights, and I no longer feel the need to drown my despair in drink. I am happy. Our daughter is utterly angelic, such a pleasant child to have around now. The chestnut ringlets frame her chubby face, and a podgy fist is curled upon her mother's breast.

Everything is so peaceful and quiet now. And I am so happy.

The past two years, with all their intense drama and the trauma, the chaos and the noise, are now just a distant memory. My family life is perfect at last.

It took a lot of courage, doing what I did. Killing my wife and my daughter, that is. But now I can see it was worth it. Look how peaceful and beautiful they are, how they both sleep.

I am happy. I am finally happy.

Organ Donor

When I applied for my driving licence and filled in the organ donor card (waste not, want not), I never thought, even for a moment, that I would be a donor so soon. I also never thought that my organs would be harvested whilst I was still alive – and conscious. I have never thought it possible to still live for a good quarter of an hour after having had the liver, stomach, pancreas and kidneys removed.

And I have never thought that my organs would be eaten by my abductors, instead of being used for transplants. Eaten raw and bloody, as soon as they have been removed from my body...

The Fruitcake

"Good afternoon, Mrs Wilkinson!", I greet the ancient-looking woman standing in front of the Reception desk. "What's it to be this week then?", I ask, eyeing the plastic carrier bag she just put on the counter. "It's only a fruitcake today, dear" she says smiling coyly with thin and withered lips, just like every week, to which I reply, also just like every week, "Oh, thank you, Mrs Wilkinson, you spoil us rotten, you know exactly what we like!"...

Mrs Wilkinson, frail, a touch senile, utterly delightful, brings in a homemade cake (usually fruitcake) every week to the local Police station. And she has done so for the past 35 years or so. Nobody really remembers how it started, although the most senior lads seem to recall how, when they first joined up, have heard from others that a long time ago, Mrs Wilkinson made a vow of weekly cakes *in perpetuum* after a bobby helped her find her lost (or was it stolen?) family heirloom (or was it her engagement ring?). Or something like that. Not that it matters, anyway. Mrs Wilkinson is a woman of her word. Week in, week out, Mrs Wilkinson comes in at the front desk with a plastic carrier and drops off a cake for us. The same polite exchange, the same dialogue:

"I hope you like it, dear", she says, in her reedy voice. And the ritual continues: "I have to go back to my Charles now, I have left him repotting the azaleas/tidying the greenhouse/getting the washing in, and you know what he's like, making more work for me than helping me, I tell you, one day dear, one day I will bloody kill him!", her voice with a touch of frustration, her arthritic hands raised towards the sky. To which the usual reply comes "Aw, I am sure he means well, Mrs Wilkinson, thank you for the cake, watch where you go, ta-ra!"... And off she goes, in her old and faded raincoat, and her little silk scarf, and decades of life (and weekly baking) weighing her small frame.

Months pass, and one sunny afternoon, Mrs Wilkinson presents herself as usual at the front desk, and I happen to be on duty, and I greet her with the usual smile, but today there are two plastic carrier bags on the counter. Mrs Wilkinson sounds a bit out of breath, and her face is flushed. "It's fruitcake again, dear", she says, pointing towards the bags, signalling me to have a look inside while she's catching her breath. I open one of the carriers, and inside is a head. A human head, that someone hastily half-wrapped in newspaper. At least I think it is, underneath that bloody mess. I feel my knees giving way, and my mouth fills with saliva, my jaws are tightening: I am going to be sick. I am heaving, trying to suppress my vomit, and I hit the emergency button, I summon my colleagues, I need my colleagues here with me, to see, to confirm that I am not losing my mind...

"That's Charles, dear!", Mrs Wilkinson quips. "The cake's in the other bag. It's fruitcake, I hope you will like it. Charles, here – she points at the bag in my paralysed hands - I told you that one day I would bloody kill him, didn't I?? I am a woman of my word..."

Message in a Bottle

Ever since I was a child, I have suffered with a rather peculiar – and at times damn right obnoxious – neurological condition: I fall asleep. As in… I fall asleep whenever… wherever… My brain takes its breaks (which are very fleeting, to be fair) pretty much whenever it feels like it. The number of times I fell asleep in the middle of a lesson at school, or later during an exam at the university… or dropped off my feet whilst shopping in the supermarket… I know it sounds funny, but believe me when I say that it wasn't as such when I once fell asleep during a love making session. The frustrating thing is, I can't help it, I can't control when or where I have these episodes.

The reason I am writing this however, is that it turns out that I don't just control when/where I fall asleep, but now it seems that I can't control when I wake up either. When, and – mostly disturbing – where I wake up...

I beg you to keep reading this, and not dismiss it as fiction or attention seeking behaviour. I am desperate, and I will explain why in a moment, just please bear with me, and keep reading...

All I know is that one day I was walking home from the shops, (I am not sure when this was, because I have either lost track of time since, and/or time flows differently now – you will see why in a minute) and I've had another sleep 'attack'. Nothing unusual so far, I know. However, when I woke up, I didn't recognise the things around me, the streets and the buildings looked all strange, everything was half destroyed like it's been in a terrible war, and the light... well, the light seemed different too, I know this sounds mad, but everything looked rather grey, sad and apocalyptic. It wasn't long until I saw military patrols roaming the area, and it all felt weird because they were dressed in uniforms like the Nazi used to wear. I have figured that there must be some sort of re-enactment convention, or perhaps a film was being shot and they were all actors of sorts, but those guns they were carrying looked real enough... Especially when this woman who got stopped by a patrol, got shot in the head execution style, and died some 300 metres away from where I was standing... Needless to say, I was in shock after witnessing that, and all my alarm bells started ringing... I ran, trying to leave this scene behind, and fortunately I reached a road which I somewhat recognised, because it looked vaguely like the area where my house was, and managed to find the building which I figured to be my place...

I know that you think that this was all a dream, a nightmare experienced during my sleep attack, but please believe me when I say that all this was real, and even though it doesn't make any sense, I am trying to explain everything. Please understand I don't have much time, so I might skip some details, and I know this story defies all logic but please, keep on reading...

So I found my house and I let myself in, but it looked all different inside, and in what was the big bedroom, I was shocked to find my dear father. Let it be known that my father died a very long time ago, when I was only a child. And now I am staring right at him, he looks a lot older, perhaps the way he would have looked had he not died some three decades ago, but his eyes... well, his eyes don't appear their usual soft and kind, they seem cold and steely, and it all looks wrong, wrong, wrong... I have tried to speak to him, but he doesn't know me, he is very alarmed and angry with me, a stranger barging into his home pretending that they are his son, go away before I call the Militia, he shouted at me, and I felt I was losing my mind.

In retrospect, now I am thinking that if I were a small girl encountering a talking rabbit and attending a weird tea party, I would have been Alice in Wonderland, but I assure you this is not a bed time story, and there were no croquet games or tea parties involved. The military regime was real, IS real, they kill people on the spot, and now they are after me because I am a stranger, an outlander. My family don't know me, it is as if I was never born, and not only that I don't belong here, but everybody wants to annihilate me, and I am running out of hiding places. Very few buildings are still standing, there's smoke and dust, hunger and chaos. I don't have much time to sit and write this, so please believe me, and try to find out a way to help me, because I don't know how to get back to my old life, and I am in mortal danger. I am leaving this note here, in a bottle near the spot I woke up in, a place which I try to visit as often as I can safely do, hoping to be able to find my way back. Please help me.

Yours faithfully,

Edward S, Jones

Another Stourport-on-Severn,

Another United Kingdom

Another 2019

The Arrival

"Come on, come on people, a bit more organisation here, please!", Agatha clapped her hands rapidly.

It was always chaos getting prepared for an arrival.

It wasn't even dawn yet, the sky was still inky, and the air was fresh.

"Oscar! Oscar!! Come here, boy! Has anybody seen Oscar?" she asked, raising her voice over the hubbub.

Coming to think of it, she hadn't seen him since yesterday evening.

Tom shrugged and walked past, with his little brother in tow.

"Are you going to put some trousers on, young man? Today??", she sighed exasperated. She left the kitchen and stood on the porch, her gaze piercing the darkness in search of Oscar.

Lovely dog, Oscar. A liver and white Springer Spaniel, proficient gun dog, full of beans as well as love. With a mind of his own, though. Often went off to do what he wanted, when he wanted.

Goodness knows where he is, thought Agatha, but if he's not back really soon, we will have to go without him.

"Aggie, have you seen my hair ribbons?", a teenage girl with a mop of unruly strawberry curls appeared in the doorway.

"They are where you left them", Agatha volunteered.

"Uughh!", the strawberry curls shook with frustration. "I can't go like this, I look like a right tramp", they continued.

"Well, there's some scissors in the drawer, Max", said Agatha with a glint of mischief in her eye, "I am only happy to solve this problem for you..."

"Ughhh!!!" Max groaned in protest and retreated into the kitchen.

The sky had a plume of violet spreading on the horizon now. They need to hurry. She went back in.

"Tom, Elliot, Max, Angela, Tony!" she called out, "We really need to hurry, come on! Ready or not!"

Her family members appeared one by one, gathering all around the old massive kitchen table.

"Right, quick inspection", Agatha looked them up and down,

"Glad to see you got your trousers on Anthony, at last, and Max - your hair looks acceptable" ("Hmphh", Max rolled her eyes at the remark).

"Has anyone seen Oscar? Where in the God's name is that flea bag, we'll have to go without him now", Agatha sighed.

Outside, the stars disappeared, and the sky was catching fire. The dawn chorus started, and the hills lit up with the blessing of a new day.

"My hat, where's my hat, right", Agatha coquettishly pinned her ancient, but still pretty summer hat on as she stood in front of the mirror, and gave her cheeks a quick pinch.

George always loved seeing her in this hat. It's what she wore on their first date, many many years ago. George - the love of her life. He is coming back home today. He is coming back for good. She couldn't wait.

"Angela, shoes, now!! You can't go to greet George in bare feet, girl, go and put your shoes on, we aren't going to Woodstock, you can't embarrass me like this!"

The first rays of sunshine broke through, the warmth and light engulfing the hills.

"Oscar!!" she called out once more. Well, she thought, they will have to go to fetch George without him. Bloody headstrong hound. But she knew, deep in her heart, that as soon as her George is home, the dog will come running. Oscar has always been George's. And a dog never forgets.

"OK, if we don't set off now, we are going to be late. We don't want to keep George waiting. Gather round, quick!" Her heart was pounding with nerves and excitement.

Butterflies doing summersaults in her tummy, just like before her first dates with George. God, he missed him so.

They held hands, and with a "Ready" nod they closed their eyes. "George, here we come!"

With a swish, Agatha and her family appeared in the hospice room: the air where they stood - shimmering like specks of dust in the sunlight. On the bed, an old man, emaciated and unconscious, was breathing his last, with each gasp his life ebbing away.

Not long now.

And on top of his feet, an indentation in the sheets: a spectral Oscar wagging his tail, his loving eyes locked on to his master.

He hadn't moved from George's bed since last night, lovingly waiting, patiently longing. A dog never forgets.

The Summoning

Radna heard the call, and felt the compelling pull. He had to leave his lair and manifest himself in physical form (although it hurt a lot, and it wiped him out for days after). The girl was summoning him. Again. This was the third time this week, and it was only Thursday. *Dark Lord help me*, he muttered under his breath.

"I am here, mistress Emily, and Radna is my name, at your service", *again*, he thought ruefully whilst he flamboyantly bowed to her, with feigned deference.

"Hm, what took you so long?", the girl pursed her lips, without even looking at him - her thumbs were dancing on her mobile phone's screen, tap-tapping. Emily was barely 15, had freckles, wore braces and had full control over a demon. Namely Radna. Him.

"I did come as soon as I heard your call, ...Mistress", bowed again Radna. He still struggled to utter the word "Mistress" in front of her, even after all this time. He struggled, of course, because he had only so many gritted teeth, and only so much spite and anger to pronounce it with. (*Count to ten, breathe...* he thought) "What is it to be today, o the great one, another zit to be vanquished? Or is it Algebra homework?"

He was seething. Nobody could really blame him for being so furious. Him, the Fierce Radna, torturer of souls, great demon of the Lower Hell, older than the Universe, at the beck and call of a... snotty little girl. It was humiliating. It was excruciating. He knew the other demons were laughing behind his back. He was losing his reputation, bit by bit, chipped away by her each and every summoning, by her stupid little chores she had for him... And she wore *braces*. And she had *freckles*, for Darkness' SAKE!

Alas, he couldn't fight it. He was helpless. She had that wretched amulet, always around her neck on a chain – and for as long as that was the case, he belonged to her. *At her beck and bloody call*, he lamented. Yes, he tried (and failed) numerous times before to trick her into taking the amulet off. To no avail though: she became his owner when she found the damn old trinket, and decided to wear it. Previous owners were a lot kinder, Radna remembered bitterly – they usually had their simple and predictable wishes, like extreme riches, social status, romantic partners. Very... low-maintenance. Mind you, they were also a lot older than her, you could say even wiser, in a way... Perhaps less self-entitled, too? Masters – and indeed ...mistresses these days aren't what they once were, Radna mused ruefully.

"Today I would like you to sort out my socks", Emily's prissy voice interrupted his reminiscing, as she was playing with the silver amulet hanging from her neck. "In colour order", the girl blinked, flashing a sadistic little smile.

"Done", Radna said, as a bit more of him died inside, after he used his mighty demonic powers to alter not only the space, but the very essence of the sock drawer. Because, after all, what's a most powerful demon to do on a Thursday afternoon, for hell's sake??? (*Breathe, be patient*, he told himself, *breathe, count to ten*)

"Would you like me to sort out your jewellery too now, Mistress? Perhaps to include the lovely amulet you currently wear, o great one?" he smiled, slyly. *Well, no harm in trying*, he thought.

"Ha ha ha, nice try, Demon", the girl chuckled in amusement. "You're too cute, always thinking that you can make me take it off... aww". *There! That patronising tone.* Radna felt his blood boiling. "Very well, Mistress" he bowed, doing his best to hide his seething anger, "In this case, may I be excused now?" *Not that I usually sit with my feet up, waiting for your call*, he silently added. He was busy. His workload in Hell was... well... diabolical. Nobody had time for going up and down, up and down, at this little girl's every whim.

"Hmmm... Let's see, what else..." Emily looked around the room, searching for other ways of destroying his pride. Of killing him slowly. And painfully. "Ah! I know!" she clapped her hands in victory. *Uh-oh, I know that look*, thought Radna. "How about Margot?! We haven't done anything to that little maggot turd for a while, have we?" Emily's eyes lit up with excitement. *No, we haven't, poor Margot-Maggot. And you can't live with yourself, if you don't torment your poor little sister every other day, can you?* Radna's heart sank.

"Well! What shall it be today for the Maggot? Mmmm how about..." Emily took a moment to think, scrunching her face, "How about... a big fat tripping down the stairs!" she exclaimed, excitedly. "At school! In view of all of her friends!! Flashing knickers, and everything!" The evil little chuckle gave Radna the chills.

"Of course, Mistress, but are you sure this is what you want? Maggot... err Margot IS your little sister, and she loves you, she..."

"Bup bup bup!" she interrupted him with her index finger in the air, which she brought slowly to her lips: "NO. ARGUING."

"Yes.... Mistress" *Damn it! Damn YOU!* Radna could scream with anger and frustration. "As you wish... Mistress".

This was Radna's least favourite type of job. Emily had a profound disdain for her little sister, and she used him now to cause Margot a plethora of accidents, misfortunes and humiliations on a regular basis. His soul died a bit each and every time he had to be the agent of Emily's sadism. Margot was... innocent. She was sweet. And she adored her big sister. And the more she loved Emily, the more Emily hated her. Poor thing, she definitely deserved better, Radna was sure of it. HE deserved better! *Aaarghhhhhh!* He screamed inside. He felt so ...dirty. He didn't want to think about it. He most certainly didn't want to talk about it.

A couple of weeks passed, and Radna hadn't heard the summon. Not that he missed it, or Emily, for that matter. But this silence.... *This silence is suspect*, he couldn't shake the feeling that something was brewing. Emily still had the amulet, and she was well, as far as he could tell. She was working on something. She was planning and scheming... *I wonder what she's got in store?* But Radna didn't have the chance to finish his thought, and Emily summoned him. *Aaarghh, damn it!*

"I am here, mistress Emily, and Radna is my name, at your service. You called?" the fiery halo materialised in Emily's pink bedroom.

Emily had a serious look on her face. *Uh-oh*, Radna felt like a school boy in the headmaster's office, about to get a severe reprimand.

"Yes, I have. Duh. I call, you come", said Emily matter of fact. "I had a thought" she continued. *Here we go, I thought I could smell burning.* "You are obligated to fulfil my every wish, correct?" *Don't I know it*, he nodded bitterly. "Well, how about we do away with the middle man?"

"Sorry, the middle what? ...Mistress?" *What the hell is she on about, are we doing riddles now?*

Emily rolled her eyes with exaggerated impatience.

"I have power over you. YOU do everything I want."

No kidding. As if I needed reminding.

"How about YOU give ME the power to do what YOU do for me ME?"

Huh?

"Mistress Emily... just to clarify... You want me to make you... someone like... Me??"

Semantics: very important.

"Yes, exactly that." Emily nodded resolutely.

Oooh, interesting, verrrry interesting indeed, thought Radna for a moment. *Oh, you clever little thing, oh yes, how didn't I think about it?? It's perfect, it's genius, of course...*

"Of course, Mistress Emily. Streamlining the process is undoubtedly the way to go" he said innocently. He could hardly contain his rising excitement. *Keep it cool, keep it calm, don't rejoice just yet...*

"Exactly. So, chop-chop. Now, if you please." Not that anything he had to do for her EVER pleased him. Only this time... *Radna, you old sod, the wheel has finally turned for you!*

With a beaming smile, Radna bowed (*for the last time – yes!!!*) and snapped his fingers. And just like that, in an instant, his torment came to an end. Emily got pulled into the depths of Hell, a demon herself, just like Radna, with incontestable powers. (Because, you know – semantics: very important.) Radna was free. FREE!!! At last.

***

"Emily, I miss you" Margot's little face was blotched from crying. Her fingers wrapped around her big sister's old necklace she now wore. That's all they found of Emily. Just her necklace. As if ...the ground had swallowed her.

Emily heard the call, and felt the compelling pull. She had to leave her lair and manifest herself in physical form (although it hurt a lot, and it wiped her out for days after). The girl was summoning her. Again. This was the third time this week, and it was only Thursday. *Dark Lord help me*, she muttered under her breath.

A Victorian Funeral

The mid November, ice cold rain was falling from a murky sky over the little village. A clump of bare trees stood mournfully on the left, with melancholy limbs piercing the wet, gloomy air as the cortege passed by. Somewhere in the distance, unseen in the wintry fog, crows could be heard, their hoarse caws carrying a sombre echo.

The carriage was drawn by two black horses, their skin steaming in the cold, and their slow clip-clop punctuating the shrinking distance towards the cemetery. The coffin was simple and unadorned - a stout six feet elm, lined with tufted red fabric, and a black silk velvet pall draped over it.

Two sturdy mutes, dressed in black and carrying staffs swathed in black crepe, were leading the procession, their beards dripping with rain. Behind, the wife: a veiled silhouette, like a broken-hearted dark spectre gliding next to her young son. Further back, the procession consisted of less than a mere handful of distant relatives and family friends. Slowly, slowly, one foot in front of the other, they walked in silence, stepping through the muddy puddles of the road, their shoes taking in the cold, unforgiving water.

The procession reached the crossroads at the heart of the village, where they stopped, momentarily. The two mutes threw a couple of coins, which landed with a dull thud on the pitiful grassy triangle in the middle. The little boy – barely six years old, thin, sickly looking and pale, walking gingerly favouring his left leg – looked up to his mother, trying to catch a glimpse of her face. His mother was shrouded in her bulky widow's weeds, with her veil so thick, it was concealing her face entirely. And he knew that the veil was concealing much more than just her features... The boy couldn't tell if she was crying or not, and for a moment he felt he was walking beside a statue covered in black dust sheets.

They reached the small village cemetery, where in between crumbling and uneven headstones, lay a dug out hole, like a mid-slumber yawn. The fog was getting thicker, and the boy saw the vicar's silhouette, waiting by the graveside, whilst a second shadow, that of a hunchback, was slouched on a spade further back. The latter was unmistakably the grave digger, the sexton, the rather monstrous looking, filthy crookback, deaf and mute from birth, whose unintelligent eyes were buried within a pock marked, ugly face. Every now and then, he would turn his deformed trunk away from the group, so he could surreptitiously take a swig from a liquor bottle. The boy could smell the brute's rancidness from where he stood.

We commit this body to the ground.... Earth to earth, dust to dust, ashes to ashes.... Alleluia... The funeral lasted only a matter of minutes, with the ancient vicar mumbling hurriedly through a pared-down service – his arthritis was made worse by the cold and the rain; and with a bad chest lately, home by his fireplace was the only place he wanted to be. The few mourners left quickly too, after murmuring their empty words of condolences to the widow. The mutes lowered the coffin in to the grave, and one of them went to tap the deaf sexton on his shoulder: their usual wordless gesture of stop your drinking, time to work now, we are done here. And with a curt bow of their heads towards the widow and her son, they turned the hearse and steered the horses back towards the village.

Then everything fell silent again.

The widow breathed out heavily and stooped to grab a handful of wet dirt from the little mound at the edge of the grave. She squeezed it hard in her gloved hand then threw it in, the little boy following her example. The two thuds as the mud hit the coffin startled him slightly, so he instinctively reached and grabbed his mother's hand.

The sexton shuffled towards them, and without waiting for them to leave, or indeed to claim a moment's silence, he started shovelling the dirt back into the hole.

Scrape, plop, scrape, plop, thud. Scrape, plop, thud, scrape, plop, thud.

The boy felt his mother's body stiffen.

Scrape, plop, thud. Scrape, thud, plop, thud, thud, thud.

The sexton was working fast, and the coffin was almost covered in dirt.

Thud, thud, thud.

The thuds were getting quieter, dampened by the increasing layer of soil on the coffin. The boy looked up to his mother, with big, scared eyes; she gave a little yelp, and put her free hand across her mouth.

The deaf-mute grave digger, oblivious in his world of eternal silence, continued to shovel dirt into the grave.

The thuds became quieter and less frantic.

Thud. Silence. *Thud.*

The boy squeezed his mother's hand, terrified.

Thud.

The woman went to gesture the sexton to stop, but paused midway – her boy was shaking in terror, pulling at her arm.

"Mummy, don't", he begged her, with tears in his eyes. "Please don't.... Let's go home... He can't harm us anymore..."

Nature is Beautiful

The little badger cub was lost. He'd never been so far away from the family sett, and he found himself all alone. The night was eerily quiet, and a large, cold moon was watching the stillness of the world. A mild frost was covering the shrubs, and made everything glitter. The ground was hard and very cold still, but the new vegetation was slowly breaking through, with the promise of a long awaited spring renewal.

From nowhere, the fox pounced.

The badger cub felt sharp, strong teeth closing over the back of his neck, like a vice. His terrified screams pierced the dark.

The grip was fierce, and he fought, trying to break loose: but it was in vain.

He screamed, and screamed, louder and louder. Will my mother come and help? The fox's jaws were so strong, and it hurt so much. His screams became frantic, blood-curdling, filling up the night with terror, with pain, with death.

Then everything fell abruptly silent.

The fox barked, triumphant: my cubs will eat tonight.

31

Printed in Great Britain
by Amazon

26073047R00020